# The Origin of Gods

希臘羅馬神話故事 ❶

# 諸神的起源　The Origin of Gods

Original Story by Thomas Bulfinch
Rewritten by Jeff Zeter
Illustrated by Ludmila Pipchenko
Designer: Eonju No
Translated by Jia-chen Chuo
Printed and distributed by Cosmos Culture Ltd.
Tel: 02-2365-9739
Fax: 02-2365-9835
http://www.icosmos.com.tw
Publisher:Value-Deliver Culture Ltd.

Photo Credits:
Zeus and Metis © Image Click; Gage © Istituto Geografico De Agostini;
Nike © Istituto Geografico De Agostini; Temple of Olympus © 2003 Euro
Photo Service Co., Ltd; Oceanus © 2003 Euro Photo Service Co., Ltd
All images are imported through Image Korea Agency Co., Ltd.

# Welcome to the World of Mythology

Mythology gives you interesting explanations about life and satisfies your curiosity with stories that have been made up to explain surprising or frightening phenomena. People throughout the world have their own myths. In the imaginary world of mythology, humans can become birds or stars. The sun, wind, trees, and the rest of the natural world are full of gods who often interact with humans.

Greek and Roman mythology began more than 3,000 years ago. It consisted of stories first told by Greeks that lived on the shores of the Mediterranean Sea. In Italy the Romans would later borrow and modify many of these stories.

Most of the Greek myths were related to gods that resided upon the cloud—shrouded Mount Olympus. These clouds frequently could create a mysterious atmosphere on Mount Olympus. The ancient Greeks thought that their gods dwelt there and had human shapes, feelings, and behavior.  The Greeks and the Romans built temples, offered animal sacrifices, said prayers, performed plays, and competed in sports to please their humanlike gods on Mount Olympus.

*How the world came into being in the first place?*
*Why is there night and day?*
*How did the four seasons come into existence?*
*Where do we go after we die?*

Reading Greek and Roman mythology can help us understand the early human conceptions of the world. Since many Western ideas originated with the Greeks and Romans, you will benefit from taking a look into the mythology that helped to shape those ancient cultures. Understanding their mythology will give you an interesting view of the world you live in.

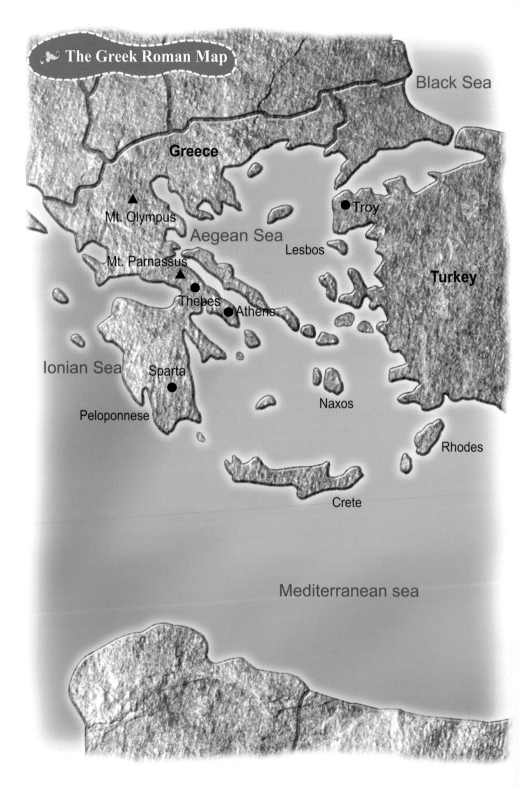

This book tells you about the birth of gods. The world began in a great darkness, no sky, mountains, and humans. It was called Chaos. Then, one day, a goddess, called Gaea was born from a seed of life.

With Uranus, son of Chaos, Gaea gave birth to many children, including Cyclopes and Hundred Handed Ones who had as many as one hundred hands. Because of the ugliness of these sons, Uranus, however, confined them to the world deep down. Gaea was outraged at this and begged Cronos to kill Uranus. Thus, Cronos replaced Uranus as king.

However, Cronos was afraid that one of his offspring would become his rival. In an attempt to avoid this, Cronos swallowed all of his children. His wife Rhea was frustrated, and when she gave birth to Zeus, she saved him, by tricking Cronos into swallowing a stone instead of Zeus.

After Zeus came back, as a fully-grown man, he gave a potion to his father, making him throw up his swallowed brothers. Then, Zeus and his brothers pulled together to get avenge on Cronos. Although the war was hard and long, Zeus was victorious. Zeus became the god of earth and heaven, ruling over all gods.

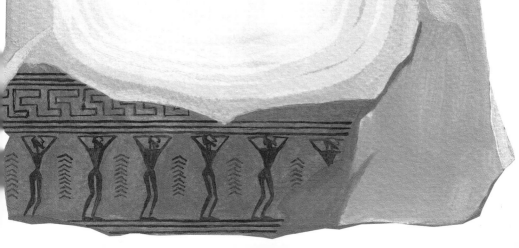

**Uranus:** The father of heaven

**Gaea:** The first goddess

## Titans:
The children of Uranus and Gaea

**Rhea:** The wife of Cronus

**Cronus:** The father of Zeus

**Hundred Handed Ones:** The monsters with one hundred hands

**Cyclopes:** The one-eyed monsters

**Zeus:** The king of the gods

**Poseidon:** The god of the sea

**Hades:** The god of the Underworld

**Hera:** The queen of the gods, and the goddess of marriage

**Demeter:** The goddess of corn, grain, and the harvest

**Hestia:** The goddess of the hearth

# Contents

In old Greece,

little Icamus and his father

sat on a mountain.

They looked up at the stars

in the night sky.

"Dad, can you tell me the story again?"

"What story?" asked his father.

"The story of the gods,

and the beginning of time,"

answered Icamus.

"OK. I'll tell you one more time."

# The Origin of Gods

Long, long ago,
there were no people or animals.
There were no trees or plants.
There were no oceans or lakes.
There were no mountains or deserts.
In fact,
there was no Earth at all.
There was only Chaos,
and nothing else.

Chaos was very messy.

Everything was mixed up.

But the seeds of life were in Chaos.

Then the mixed-up parts divided.

The gas part was the lightest.

It became the sky.

The rocky part was heavier.

It became the earth.

And the wet part was the heaviest.

It became the water.

Then, a new part came.

This part was called Gaea.

She was the goddess
of making new life.

Gaea wanted to make the Earth beautiful.
On land,
she made animals.
In the water,
she made fish.
And in the air,
she made birds.

Chaos had a son called Uranus.

When he grew up, he became the Sky Father.

Gaea and Uranus had many children together.

First, they had children called the Titans.

Some were wise and some were not.

They were all very powerful, though.

The Titans ruled the Earth for a long time.

04

# Gaea

Gaea is often called the Earth Mother.

She came long before the other gods.

In old Greek, people prayed to her.

They believed all life came from Gaea.

Her statues first appeared thousands of years ago.

These old statues always look very chubby.

Gaea

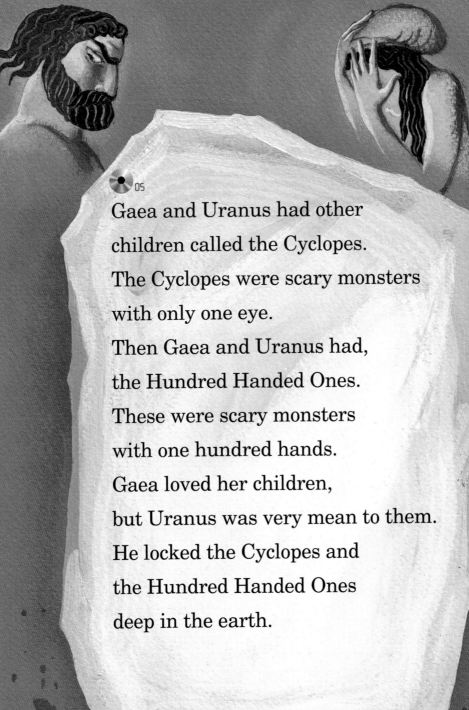

Gaea and Uranus had other
children called the Cyclopes.
The Cyclopes were scary monsters
with only one eye.
Then Gaea and Uranus had,
the Hundred Handed Ones.
These were scary monsters
with one hundred hands.
Gaea loved her children,
but Uranus was very mean to them.
He locked the Cyclopes and
the Hundred Handed Ones
deep in the earth.

The youngest, and boldest,
of the Titans was Cronus.
One night, Gaea talked quietly with him.
"Son, your father is terrible!" she said,
"He put my children deep in the earth.
We must stop him!"
"But how, Mom?" asked Cronus.

Gaea gave Cronus a big knife.
Late at night,
he hid in Uranus's bedroom.
When Uranus fell asleep,
Cronus attacked him.
Cronus won the fight.
He threw his father
into the sea.

So Cronus became
a powerful Titan ruler.
He married Rhea, another Titan.
"Hmm" thought Cronus one day,
"Now I am the most powerful Titan.
But my children will be
stronger than me one day.
They will want to rule, too.
I must stop this."

# Titans

In the Greek stories,

the Titans were the first gods.

In all, there were 12 Titans.

They grew very large.

In English, "titan" means very large.

Each of the Titans ruled over

a part of nature.

For instance,

Oceanus ruled

over the water.

The English word

"ocean" comes

from this.

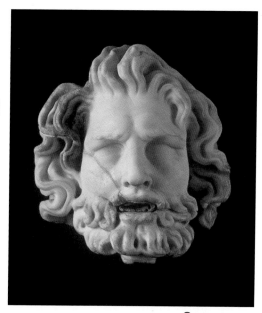

Oceanus

GULP

09 Cronus thought about
his problem for a long time.
Then, one day, he had an idea.
"I'll just eat my kids!"
thought Cronus, "Yes, that's it.
My children will never challenge me!
What a wonderful idea!
I'm not just powerful. I'm smart, too!"

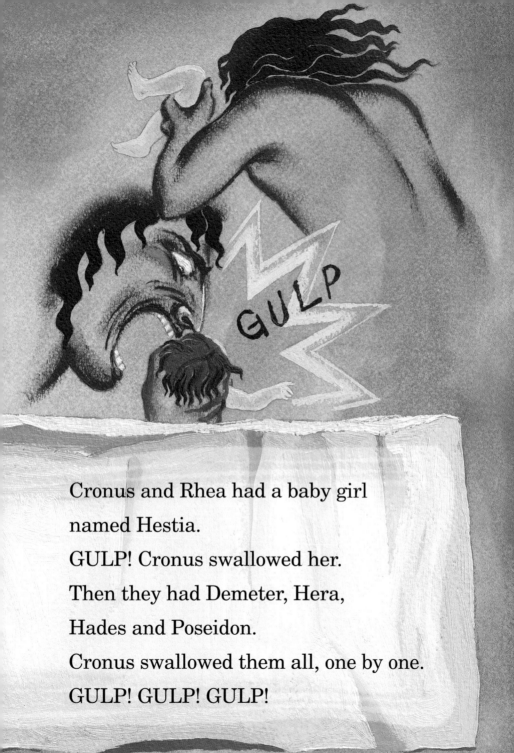

Cronus and Rhea had a baby girl
named Hestia.
GULP! Cronus swallowed her.
Then they had Demeter, Hera,
Hades and Poseidon.
Cronus swallowed them all, one by one.
GULP! GULP! GULP!

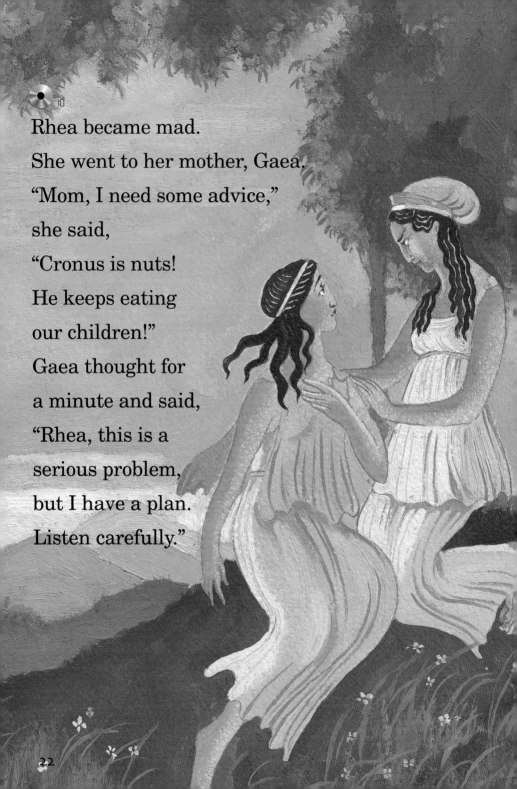

Rhea became mad.
She went to her mother, Gaea.
"Mom, I need some advice,"
she said,
"Cronus is nuts!
He keeps eating
our children!"
Gaea thought for
a minute and said,
"Rhea, this is a
serious problem,
but I have a plan.
Listen carefully."

# The Birth of Zeus

Cronus and Rhea had

another son named Zeus.

He was very strong and healthy.

Rhea carefully followed Gaea's advice.

First, she wrapped a rock with a blanket.

Rhea gave the rock, not Zeus, to Cronus.

"This kid is as hard as a rock!" said Cronus,

"Oh, well. At least he'll never take my power!"

Then Cronus swallowed the rock.

Gaea told Rhea about a cave in the mountains.

Rhea hid little Zeus in the cave.

A kind nymph-goat named Amaltheia lived there.

Amaltheia and other nymphs
took good care of Zeus.

Years passed, and Zeus became a strong young god. He married Metis, a Titan's daughter.

When Zeus returned, his mother was very happy,
but his father wasn't.

One day, Rhea came to Zeus.

"Cronus ate my children many years ago.
I miss them so much," she said.

"I'm sure they are still alive," said Zeus,
"I can help you. I'll bring them back."

Then Zeus made a plan all night.

The next day, Zeus met Cronus.
"You are the strongest
and wisest Titan," said Zeus,

"I will pour some
special wine for you."
"Well, Zeus, I'm glad you think so.
Yes, please pour me some wine, boy."
But it wasn't wine.
It was a magic drink.

Cronus drank it quickly.

"Ugh, I don't feel very well.

I think I'm going to throw up,"

Cronus said. BELCH!

Then, one by one, his children came out.

Hestia, Demeter, Hera, Hades and Poseidon.

All his children came out.

Finally,
the rock came out, too.
"I ate a rock?" asked Cronus.
"So that's why my stomach
always hurts."

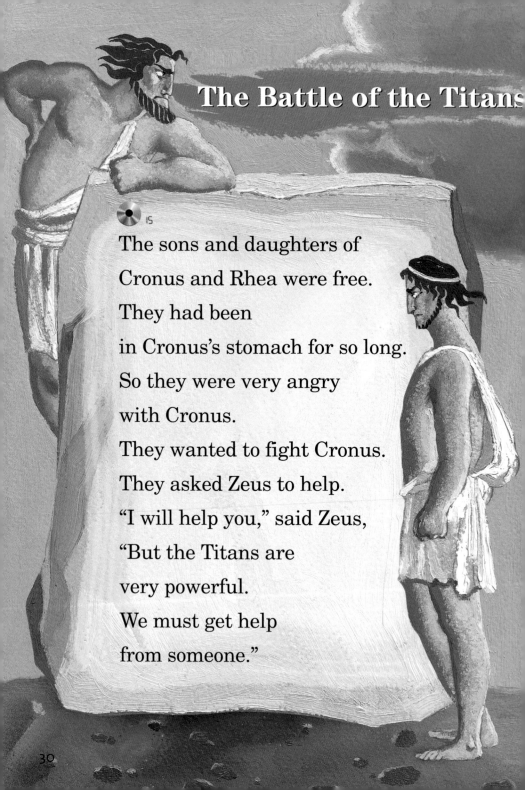

The sons and daughters of
Cronus and Rhea were free.
They had been
in Cronus's stomach for so long.
So they were very angry
with Cronus.
They wanted to fight Cronus.
They asked Zeus to help.
"I will help you," said Zeus,
"But the Titans are
very powerful.
We must get help
from someone."

That night, Zeus went to see his mother.
"Mom, Cronus is a mean leader.
We must stop him. But how?"
Rhea looked into the future.
"Victory will be very difficult," said Rhea,
"You must free the Cyclopes and
the Hundred Handed Ones.
Uranus put them deep in the earth.
You can fight Cronus with their help."

So Zeus went deep into the earth.

It was hot and smelly.

There was fire everywhere.

Finally, he reached the center of the earth.

"I am here to free you!" said Zeus,

"We must fight Cronus."

"Hooray!" said the Cyclopes,

"Yes, let's go!"

Zeus wanted some more help.
So he talked to the other Titans.
"I need your help to fight Cronus.
Join me. Together we can win!"
said Zeus.
Only some of the Titans joined Zeus.
But others joined Cronus.

# Styx & Nike

The Titan Oceanus controlled the water.

His daughter was Styx.

She was the goddess of a river in the underworld.

People crossed this river after they died.

One of Styx's daughters,

Nike was
the goddess
of victory.
The shoe
company,
Nike
is named
after her.

Nike

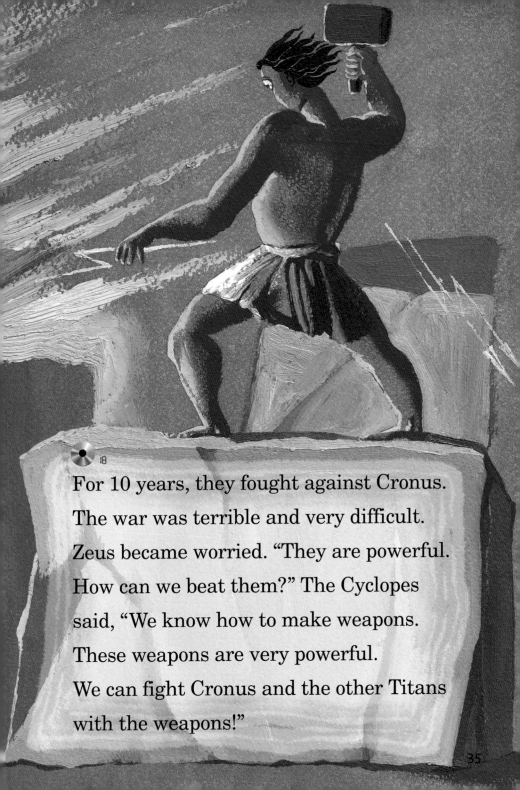

For 10 years, they fought against Cronus.
The war was terrible and very difficult.
Zeus became worried. "They are powerful.
How can we beat them?" The Cyclopes
said, "We know how to make weapons.
These weapons are very powerful.
We can fight Cronus and the other Titans
with the weapons!"

The Cyclopes gave Hades a mysterious helmet. "No one can see you when you wear this helmet."

Then, the Cyclopes gave Poseidon a trident. "You can use this trident to attack your enemies. It can also make floods, earthquakes and storms."

Finally, the Cyclopes gave Zeus a thunderbolt.
"This is the most powerful weapon of all.
But be careful. It is very dangerous!
It can destroy a mountain and even the world.
You must guard it well!"

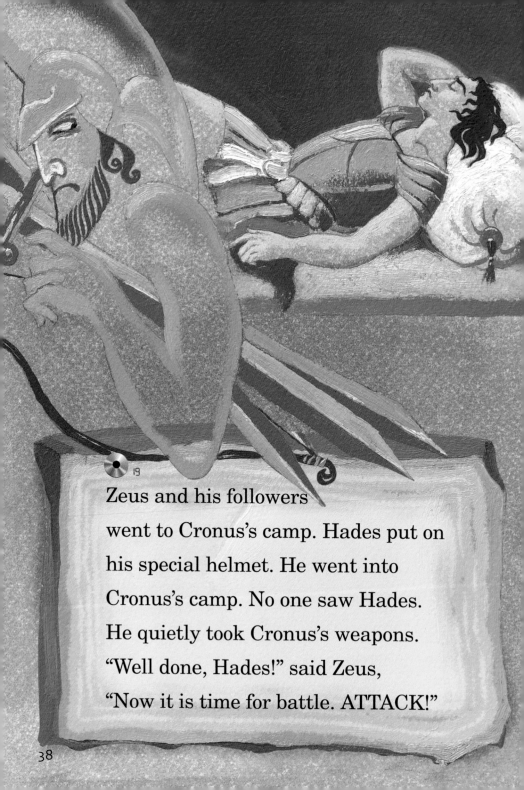

Zeus and his followers
went to Cronus's camp. Hades put on
his special helmet. He went into
Cronus's camp. No one saw Hades.
He quietly took Cronus's weapons.
"Well done, Hades!" said Zeus,
"Now it is time for battle. ATTACK!"

Zeus and his followers ran into the camp.

Cronus and the Titans were shocked.

"Zeus is attacking!" said Cronus,

"Bring me my weapons quickly!"

"I can't find them!" said a Titan,

"Where are they?"

Poseidon attacked Cronus with his trident,
but Cronus was a good fighter.
Poseidon couldn't beat Cronus alone,
then Zeus lifted his mighty thunderbolt.

The thunderbolt hit Cronus.

It knocked him over.

Again and again, Zeus threw the thunderbolt.

Finally, Cronus was defeated.

Zeus and his followers

won The Battle of the Titans.

Cronus went far away after the battle.

Zeus sent the Titans to the center
of the earth.

The Hundred Handed Ones guarded them.

Zeus shared the power with other gods.

Zeus became the god of Heaven and Earth
and the king of the gods and goddesses.

Poseidon controlled the sea.

Hades became the god
of the underworld.

In all, there were 12 gods of Olympus.
They lived on Mount Olympus in Greece.
The gods of Olympus controlled nature.
The 12 gods brought new ideas to man.

Temple of Olympus

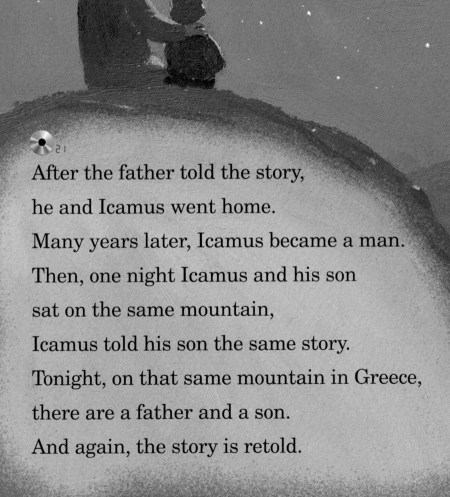

After the father told the story,

he and Icamus went home.

Many years later, Icamus became a man.

Then, one night Icamus and his son

sat on the same mountain,

Icamus told his son the same story.

Tonight, on that same mountain in Greece,

there are a father and a son.

And again, the story is retold.

# Reading Comprehension

Read the questions and choose the best answers.

1. According to Greek Roman Myths, what was the first thing to exist?

   (A) Zeus        (B) Gaea

   (C) Chaos       (D) the Earth

2. How many eyes did the Cyclopes have?

   (A) 1           (B) 2

   (C) 10          (D) 100

3. What did Cronus do to his children so they wouldn't challenge him?

(A) He sent them to Mount Olympus.

(B) He sent them to the center of the earth.

(C) He ate them.

(D) He locked them in a cage.

4. Who was the daughter of Oceanus?

(A) Styx                    (B) Hera

(C) Athena                 (D) Roberta

5. Who was Amaltheia?

(A) Zeus's mother      (B) a nymph-goat

(C) a ruler of the gods (D) Zeus's wife

Read and circle.

6. The Cyclopes and Cronus are Uranus's sons.

True          False

7. Gaea took care of little Zeus in the cave.

True          False

8. Zeus became the god of the underworld.

True          False

9. The Cyclopes gave a trident to Hades.

True          False

10. Zeus lived on Mount Olympus
in Greece.

True          False

# The Origin of Gods

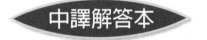

中譯解答本

卓加貞　譯

　　神話用有趣的方式說明生命，各種故事解釋各種奇異或可怕現象，滿足人們的好奇心。世界上的每個民族，都有自己的神話。在神話的奇幻世界裡，人類可以化身成鳥或星辰。太陽、風、樹木等等，自然界萬物皆充滿了和人類互動頻繁的神靈。

　　希臘和羅馬神話的出現，已超過三千年，源自居住在地中海岸的希臘人。之後，再由義大利的羅馬人所接受，並進一步改寫之。

　　希臘神話的故事，大都與雲霄上的奧林帕斯山諸神有關。雲霧常為奧林帕斯山蒙上神祕的氣氛，古希臘人認為，神明就住在山上，其形體、感情和行為舉止，無異於人。希臘人和羅馬人建立寺廟、獻祭動物、祈禳，並用戲劇和運動競賽的方式，來取悅那些住在奧林帕斯山、與人同形同性的眾神。

　　世界最初是如何形成的？
　　為什麼會有晝夜之分？
　　為什麼會有四季變化？
　　人死後將從何而去？

　　閱讀希臘羅馬神話，可以幫助我們瞭解早期人類的世界觀。又因許多西方思想乃源自於希臘人和羅馬人，故窺視希臘羅馬神話，將有助於塑造出那些古文化的真貌。瞭解這些神話的內容，將可以讓人們對這個世界別有一番趣解。

本書說明諸神之誕生。這個世界起初一片黑暗，稱為渾沌，沒有天空、山脈或人類。接著有一天，在生命的種子中，誕生出了一位名叫蓋亞的女神。

　　蓋亞和渾沌之子烏拉諾斯生下諸子，如車輪眼巨人和百手怪眾子。但由於眾子長相醜陋，就被烏拉諾斯幽禁在地底深處。蓋亞為此感到憤怒，便請求克羅納斯把烏拉諾斯殺掉，克羅納斯於是取代了烏拉諾斯成為國王。

　　然而，克羅納斯擔心子女會跟他爭權，為除後患，克羅納斯吞掉眾子，妻子莉亞深感難過。莉亞在生下宙斯時，便調包救子，讓克羅納斯吞下石頭，而非宙斯。

　　當宙斯長大成年回來後，他讓父親服下藥水，吐出吞入腹中的眾子。之後，宙斯和眾兄弟開始合力報復克羅納斯。他們打了一場漫長而艱辛的戰爭，但宙斯終究獲得了最後的勝利，並成為了天上人間的神明，統理眾神。

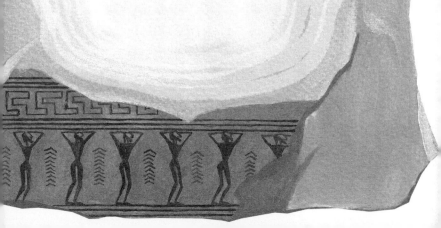

## The characters in the stories

**Uranus:** The father of heaven

**Gaea:** The first goddess

### Titans:
The children of Uranus and Gaea

**Cyclopes:** The one-eyed monsters

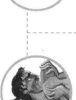

**Hundred Handed Ones:** The monsters with one hundred hands

**Cronus:** The father of Zeus

**Rhea:** The wife of Cronus

**Hestia:** The goddess of the hearth

**Demeter:** The goddess of the grain and the harvest

**Hera:** The queen of the gods

**Hades:** The god of the Underworld

**Poseidon:** The god of the sea

**Zeus:** The king of the gods

# 目錄

## p.8

在遠古的希臘，

年幼的伊卡和父親，

坐在山丘上。

他們在夜晚仰首觀星。

「爸爸，你可以再說一次那個故事嗎？」

「什麼故事？」父親問道。

「就是那個有很多神和世界起源的故事。」伊卡回答道。

「好，那我就再說一次了。」

- **Greece** [gri:s] 希臘
- **sat** [sæt] 坐
  （sit的過去式）
- **look up** [luk ʌp]
  向上看；仰望
- **again** [əˋgen] 再；又
- **god** [gɑ:d] 神
- **beginning** [brˋgɪn.ɪŋ]
  開始

## p.9

# 眾神的起源

在很久很久以前，

那時候，

人類和動物尚未出現，

也沒有樹木和植物，

沒有海洋和湖泊，

沒有山岳和沙漠。

事實上，當時連大地都還沒有出現。

那時候宇宙只是一片渾沌，

無一物存在。

- **origin** [ˋɔ:r.əd3ɪn] 起源
- **there was/were**
  [ðer wɑ:z/wɜ:] 那裡有
- **plant** [plænt] 植物
- **ocean** [ˋouʃᵊn] 海洋
- **lake** [leɪk] 湖泊
- **mountain** [ˋmauntᵊn]
  山；山脈
- **desert** [drˋzɜ:t] 沙漠
- **Earth** [ɜ:θ] 地球
- **Chaos** [ˋkeɪɑ:s]
  渾沌

**p. 10**

渾沌沒有秩序,一切糾纏不分。
但渾沌之中有生命種子。
之後,萬物區分開來。
氣體是最輕的,
它升上空變成了蒼穹。
岩石較重,變成了大地。
溼氣是最重的,變成了水。
接著,新的事物誕生了,
她是創造生命的女神,蓋亞。

- **messy** [ˈmes.i]
  雜亂的;骯髒的
- **everything** [ˈev.rɪ.θɪn]
  所有事物
- **be mixed up**
  [bi: mɪkst ʌp] 混雜
- **seed** [si:d] 種子
- **divide** [dɪˈvaɪd] 分開
- **gas** [gæs] 氣體
- **lightest** [laɪtɪ:st] 最輕的
- **rocky** [ˈrɑ:.ki] 岩石的
- **heavier** [ˈhev.ɪ:r]
  較沉重的
- **wet** [wet] 潮濕的

---

**p. 11**

蓋亞想要讓大地變得美麗。
她便於陸地上,創造各種動物,
於水中,創造魚群,
於空中,創造群鳥。

- **beautiful** [ˈbju:.tɪ.fᵊl]
  美麗的
- **air** [er] 空氣

---

**p. 12**

渾沌有一子,
名叫烏拉諾斯。
烏拉諾斯長大後,

- **grew up** [gru: ʌp]
  長大成人;成熟
- **together** [təˈgeð.ɚ]
  總合;一起

成為了天神，

並和蓋亞生出了許多子嗣。

起先，他們生下泰坦諸神。

泰坦神族的資質參差不齊，

但個個力大無比。

這些泰坦神統治了大地好長一段時間。

- **first** [ˋfɜːst] 最初；起先
- **Titan** [ˋtaɪ.tᵊn]
  （希神）泰坦
- **wise** [waɪz]
  聰明的；有智慧的
- **powerful** [ˋpaʊə.fᵊl]
  強而有力的
- **though** [ðoʊ] 然而
- **rule** [ruːl] 支配；統治
- **for a long time**
  [fə ə lɑːŋ taɪm]
  持續了一段時間

---

p. 13　( Did you know? )

# 蓋亞

蓋亞常被稱為「大地之母」，

在眾神出現之前，她早已存在。

在古希臘，人們向她祈禱，

他們相信萬物都起源於她。

她的雕像在幾千年前就已經存在了，

這些古代的人物雕刻，

大多都擁有豐腴的外型。

- **long before** [lɑːŋ bɪˋfɔːr]
  許久之前
- **other** [ˋʌð.ɚ] 其餘的
- **pray** [preɪ] 祈禱
- **believe** [bɪˋliːv] 相信
- **statue** [ˋstætʃ.uː] 雕像
- **thousands of**
  [ˋθaʊ.zᵊnts ɑːv]
  數以千計的
- **chubby** [ˋtʃʌb.i]
  豐腴的；胖乎乎的

**p. 15**

蓋亞和烏拉諾斯還生下了車輪眼巨人，
他們是可怕的獨眼怪獸。
繼之，蓋亞和烏拉諾斯生下百手怪。
他們是駭人無比的怪物。
蓋亞疼愛眾子，
但烏拉諾斯待子刻薄無情，
他把車輪眼巨人和百手怪囚禁在地底深處。

- **scary** [`ske.ri] 駭人的
- **monster** [`ma:nt.stɚ] 怪獸
- **hundred** [`hʌn.drəd] 一百的
- **mean** [mi:n] 刻薄的
- **lock** [la:k] 鎖住
- **deep** [di:p] 深深的

 **p. 16**

克羅納斯是最年輕英勇的泰坦神，
有一天晚上，
蓋亞低聲對他說：
「兒啊，你父親是個可怕的人！
他把其他的孩子打入了地底，
我們必須制止他！」
「但要怎麼做呢，母親？」
克羅納斯問道。

- **youngest** [jʌŋgɪst] 最年輕的
- **boldest** [bouldɪst] 最大膽的；最勇敢的
- **talk with** [ta:k wɪð] 與……說話
- **quietly** [kwaɪətlɪ] 安靜地
- **terrible** [`ter.ə.bl] 糟透的；可怕的
- **put** [pʊt] 放置；迫使
- **must** [mʌst] 必需

**p. 17**

蓋亞遂遞給了克羅納斯一把大刀。
夜半時分，
克羅納斯躲進父親房內。
待父親熟睡之後，

- **knife** [naɪf] 刀子
- **late** [leɪt] 晚的
- **hid** [haɪd] 藏匿
- **bedroom** [`bed.rʊm] 臥室
- **fall asleep** [fa:l əˋsli:p] 入睡

克羅納斯便起身攻擊。

他擊倒了父親，將他丟入海中。

- **attack** [ə`tæk] 攻擊
- **won** [wʌn] 勝利
  （win的過去式）
- **fight** [faɪt] 作戰
- **threw** [θru:] 扔進
  （throw的過去式）

---

 **p. 18**

克羅納斯於是成為泰坦神族的權威統治者。

他娶了另一位泰坦神莉亞。

有一天，克羅納斯心想：「現在我是最具權力威望的泰坦神，

但將來我的子嗣會比我更強壯，

他們也會想要掌權，我得想個辦法。」

- **ruler** [`ru:.lə] 統治者
- **married** [`mær.id]
  和……結婚
  （marry的過去式）
- **another** [ə`nʌð.ə]
  另一個
- **thought** [θɑ:t]
  考慮；思考
  （think的過去式）
- **one day** [wʌn deɪ]
  有一天

---

 **p. 19** (Did you know?)

# 泰坦諸神

在希臘神話中，

泰坦神是最初的第一批神，

共有十二位。

泰坦神體型巨碩，

- **in all** [ɪn ɑ:l]
  總共；總合
- **large** [lɑ:rdʒ] 巨大的
- **mean** [mi:n] 意味著
- **each** [i:tʃ]
  每一個；各別
- **part** [pɑ:rt] 部分
- **rule over** [ru:l `oʊ.və]
  統治著

在英文裡，
titan這個字就是「巨大」的意思。
每一位泰坦神
各掌管大自然的一部分，
舉例來說，大洋氏掌管水域，
英文字ocean就是從他而來的。

* **nature** [`neɪ.tʃə]
  大自然
* **for instance**
  [fɔːr `ɪn.stənts] 舉例來說

---

 p. 20

克羅納斯思忖了很久。
有一天，他靈光一現，心想：
「我就把孩子們吃掉吧！
對，就這麼辦！
這樣他們就永遠無法反抗我了！
這真是個好主意！
我不僅威力無窮，
還聰明無比啊！」

* **problem** [`prɑː.bləm]
  問題；疑問
* **have an idea**
  [hæv ən aɪ`dɪə] 有個主意
* **just** [dʒʌst] 僅；只
* **kid** [kɪd] 小孩
* **never** [`nev.ə] 絕不
* **challenge** [`tʃæl.ɪndʒ]
  挑戰
* **wonderful** [`wʌn.də.fəl]
  極好的；絕妙的
* **smart** [smɑːrt] 聰明

---

 p. 21

克羅納斯和莉亞生下一名女嬰，
名叫赫斯西雅。
咕嚕！克羅納斯吞下了她。
接著，他們生下狄蜜特、赫拉、海地士

* **gulp** [gʌlp]
  一大口吞下；吞咽聲
* **swallow** [`swɑː.loʊ]
  吞；嚥

和波賽墩。

克羅納斯也將他們全部一一吞下。

咕嚕！咕嚕！咕嚕！

- **one by one**
  [wʌn baɪ wʌn]
  一個接著一個

---

**p. 22**

莉亞氣憤不已，便跑去找母親蓋亞，

說道：「母親，請給我一些建議吧！

克羅納斯失去理智了！

他將孩子一個個吃進肚子裡！」

蓋亞想了一會兒，說道：

「莉亞，此事非同小可，

但我有個辦法，仔細聽著。」

- **mad** [mæd]
  狂怒的；極度瘋狂的
- **need** [niːd] 需要
- **advice** [ədˋvaɪs]
  忠告；建議
- **nuts** [nʌts] 發瘋
- **keep -ing** [ˋkiːp ɪŋ]
  保持（持續）某種狀態
- **for a minute**
  [fɔːr əˋmɪn.ɪt] 一秒鐘間
- **serious** [ˋsɪr.iəs] 嚴重的
- **plan** [plæn] 計畫
- **listen** [ˋlɪs.ᵊn] 聽
- **carefully** [ˋker.fᵊl.i]
  仔細地；小心地

---

**p. 23**

# 宙斯的誕生

克羅納斯和莉亞接著生下了宙斯，

宙斯生得又健康又強壯。

莉亞小心翼翼地

遵照蓋亞的指示進行計畫。

- **named** [neɪmd] 取名為
- **strong** [strɑːŋ] 強壯
- **healthy** [ˋhel.θi] 健康
- **follow** [ˋfɑː.loʊ]
  跟隨（聽從）
- **wrap** [ræp] 包裹
- **rock** [rɑːk] 石塊；岩石

首先，

她把一塊大石頭用毛毯包裹起來，

把這石頭假裝成宙斯，

交給克羅納斯。

「這孩子硬得像塊石頭！」

克羅納斯說：

「不過，

他好歹永遠都無法篡奪我的王位了！」

接著，克羅納斯便一口吞下石頭。

- **blanket** [ˋblæŋ.kɪt] 毛毯
- **as A as B** [əz e əz bi:]
  如同……一樣……
- **at least** [æt li:st] 至少
- **take** [teɪk] 取走；奪走

---

 **p. 24**

蓋亞告訴莉亞，

在某座山中有個洞穴，

莉亞便將宙斯藏身在那個洞穴裡。

洞穴裡住著一位善良的山羊女神，

名為阿瑪爾夏，

她和其他水澤女神一起

照顧宙斯長大。

- **cave** [keɪv]
  山洞；洞穴
- **nymph** [nɪmpf] 寧芙
  （居於山林水澤的仙女）
- **goat** [goʊt] 山羊
- **take good care of**
  [teɪk gʊd ker əv]
  完好的照顧

---

 **p. 25**

多年過後，

宙斯成為一位健壯的神祇。

他娶了泰坦神之女——美蒂絲。

- **year** [jɪr] 年
- **pass** [pæs] （時間）
  過去；從旁經過
- **young** [jʌŋ] 年輕

當宙斯長大後回到家，
母親莉亞歡喜不已，
父親克羅納斯卻不悅於心。
有一天，莉亞來找宙斯，對他說：
「多年多年以前，
克羅納斯吃下了我其他的孩子，
我好想念他們啊。」
宙斯說：「我想他們還活著的，
我可以幫你把他們找回來。」
宙斯於是通宵達旦地籌謀策畫。

* **return** [rɪ`tɜːn] 返回
* **miss** [mɪs] 思念
* **sure** [ʃʊr] 確信
* **still** [stɪl] 仍然
* **alive** [ə`laɪv] 存活
* **bring back** [brɪŋ bæk] 帶回來
* **make a plan** [meɪk ə plæn] 擬定計畫
* **all night** [ɔːl naɪt] 整晚

隔天，宙斯晉見克羅納斯，說道：
「泰坦神中，您是最為威猛睿智的，
讓我為您斟上一杯特別的酒吧。」
「宙斯，很高興你能這麼想，
好吧，為我斟杯酒吧，孩子。」
只不過，宙斯倒的並不是酒，
而是一種具有魔力的飲料。

* **the next day** [ðə nekst deɪ] 隔天
* **met** [miːt] 和……見面（meet的過去式）
* **wisest** [waɪzɪst] 最聰明的
* **pour** [pɔːr] 倒；注；灌
* **special** [`speʃəl] 特別的
* **wine** [waɪn] 酒
* **magic** [`mædʒɪk] 神奇的；有魔力的
* **drink** [drɪŋk] 飲料

14

p. 28

克羅納斯大口喝下。
「嗯,我覺得很不舒服,
我想我要吐了!」
克羅納斯說著,便吐了出來!
他的孩子們,也一個個被吐了出來。
赫斯西雅、狄蜜特、赫拉、海地士和波賽墩,
所有孩子都出來了。

- **drank** [dræŋk] 喝下
  (drink的過去式)
- **quickly** [ˈkwɪk.li]
  快速的
- **don't feel well**
  [doʊnt fi:l wel]
  感覺不舒服
- **be going to**
  [bi: gəʊ.ɪŋ tə] 將要……
- **throw up** [θroʊ ʌp] 嘔吐
- **belch** [beltʃ] 嘔吐聲
- **came out** [keɪm aʊt]
  出來(come out的過去式)

---

p. 29

最後,那塊石頭也被吐出來了。
「我竟吞了一顆石頭?」
克羅納斯納悶道:
「難怪我老是肚子痛。」

- **finally** [ˈfaɪ.nə.li] 終於
- **ate** [et] 吃下
  (eat的過去式)
- **stomach** [ˈstʌm.ək]
  胃;腹部
- **hurt** [hɜ:t] 疼痛

## 泰坦神之戰

p. 30

克羅納斯和莉亞的孩子們恢復了自由。
他們被困在父親的肚子裡這麼久，
心有不甘，故想起而撻伐父親。
他們去請宙斯幫忙，宙斯說：
「我會拔刀相助，但泰坦神力大無窮，
我們還需要其他援兵。」

* **battle** [ˈbæt̬.l̩] 戰爭
* **free** [friː]
  自由的；自主的
* **be angry with**
  [bi ˈæŋ.gri wɪð]
  對……感到憤怒
* **get** [get] 取得；獲得

p. 31

當晚，宙斯前去探望母親。
「母親，克羅納斯是個昏君，
我們得推翻他，但要怎麼做呢？」
莉亞掐指一算，說道：
「難有勝算。
你得先把車輪眼和百手怪放出來，
他們被烏拉諾斯關在地底下。
有他們的相助，
你才能打敗烏拉諾斯。」

* **leader** [ˈliː.də] 領導者
* **future** [ˈfjuː.tʃə] 未來
* **victory** [ˈvɪk.tər.i] 勝利
* **difficult** [ˈdɪf.ɪ.kəlt]
  困難的
* **free** [friː] 釋放

p. 32

宙斯於是來到地底深處。
地底下灼熱不堪，臭氣沖天，
到處都是火焰。
最後，他來到地心。
「我來，是為了釋放你們！」
宙斯說：
「我們要一起對抗克羅納斯。」
「太好了！」車輪眼說：
「我們就走吧！」

- **smelly** [ˋsmel.i]
  有難聞〔強烈〕氣味的
- **everywhere** [ˋev.ri.wer]
  到處
- **reach** [riːtʃ] 達到（目標）
- **center** [ˋsen.tͼ] 中心的
- **Hooray!** [huˋreɪ]
  （感嘆詞）萬歲

p. 33

宙斯需要更多幫助，
他便告訴其他泰坦神說：
「為了打敗克羅納斯，
我需要各位的幫忙！
來吧！我們只要團結，
就能打敗克羅納斯！」
然而，只有部分的泰坦神跟隨宙斯，
其他的則加入了克羅納斯的陣營。

- **join** [dʒɔɪn]
  參加；加入
- **win** [wɪn] 獲勝

**p. 34**

Did you know?

# 守誓河與奈吉

泰坦神大洋氏掌管水域，
其女為守誓河，是冥界的女河神。
人們死後，會渡過此河。
奈吉，則是守誓河的一女，
她是勝利女神，
著名的耐吉（Nike）球鞋公司，
就是以她命名的。

- **control** [kən`troʊl]
  控制；支配
- **Styx** [stɪks]
  （希臘神）守誓河
- **river** [`rɪv.ə] 河流
- **underworld**
  [ʌn.də.wɜːld]
  地獄；陰間
- **cross** [krɑːs] 越過、渡過
- **die** [daɪ] 死去
- **company** [`kʌm.pə.ni]
  公司

---

**p. 35**

眾神和克羅納斯大戰了十年，
戰況激烈，死傷慘重。
宙斯開始憂心了起來，說道：
「對手如此強大，
我們如何才能戰勝呢？」
車輪眼巨人說：
「我們能製造兵器，
用這些威力強大的兵器，
就可以打敗克羅納斯和其他泰坦神！」

- **fought** [fɑːt]
  作戰；戰鬥
  （fight的過去式）
- **war** [wɔːr] 戰爭
- **became worried**
  [bɪ`keɪm `wɜːr.id]
  變得有煩惱的樣子
- **beat** [biːt]
  戰勝（對手）；
  超越（敵手）
- **weapon** [`wep.ən] 武器

車輪眼巨人遞給海地士一頂神奇的頭盔，說道：
「戴上這個頭盔，就可以隱形。」

接著，
車輪眼巨人又給波賽墩一支三叉戟，
說道：
「用這支三叉戟來對抗敵人！
它能召喚洪水、地震和暴風雨。」

- **mysterious** [mɪˋstɪr.i.əs] 神秘的；不可思議的
- **helmet** [ˋhel.mət] 頭盔
- **no one** [noʊ wʌn] 沒有任何人
- **wear** [wer] 穿戴
- **trident** [ˋtraɪ.dənt] 三叉的
- **attack** [əˋtæk] 攻擊
- **enemy** [ˋen.ə.mi] 敵人
- **flood** [flʌd] 洪水
- **earthquake** [ˋɜːθ.kweɪk] 地震
- **storm** [stɔːrm] 風暴

最後，車輪眼巨人給宙斯一支閃電。
「這是威力最強大的兵器，
千萬小心啊，
它危險無比，足以造成山崩地裂，
請務必謹慎使用！」

- **thunderbolt** [ˋθʌn.dɚ.boʊlt] 伴有雷鳴的閃電
- **Be careful** [bi: ˋker.fəl] 使……小心
- **dangerous** [ˋdeɪn.dʒɚr.əs] 危險的
- **destroy** [dɪˋstrɔɪ] 毀壞
- **guard** [gɑːrd] 守護；防衛

### p. 38

宙斯和手下來到克羅納斯的陣營中。

海地士戴上神奇頭盔，

走進克羅納斯的軍營，無人發覺。

他悄悄拿走克羅納斯的武器。

宙斯說：「幹得好啊！

現在，開始戰鬥！進攻！」

- **follower** [ˈfɑː.lou.ɚ]
  隨從
- **camp** [kæmp]
  兵營；軍營
- **put on** [pʊt ɑːn] 戴上

---

### p. 39

宙斯和手下衝進營裡，

克羅納斯和泰坦神震驚不已。

「宙斯攻過來了！」克羅納斯說：

「快把我的兵器拿來！」

其中一位泰坦神說：

「兵器不見了！兵器在哪裡呀？」

- **be shocked** [biː ʃɑːkt]
  受驚嚇
- **shock** [ʃɑːk] 震驚；驚愕
- **quickly** [ˈkwɪk.li]
  快速地
- **find** [faɪnd] 找到

## p. 40

波賽墩以他的三叉戟對付克羅納斯。
但克羅納斯驍勇善戰，
波賽墩無法獨力擊敗他。
後來，宙斯舉起他威力十足的閃電，

- **fighter** [ˈfaɪ.tə]
  戰士；士兵
- **alone** [əˈloʊn] 單獨地
- **lift** [lɪft]
  搶；提起
- **mighty** [ˈmaɪ.ti]
  有力的；強大的

---

## p. 41

閃電擊中了克羅納斯，
將他擊倒在地。
宙斯一次次擊出閃電，
最後，克羅納斯被打敗了。
宙斯和手下，
贏得了這場與泰坦神的戰爭。

- **hit** [hɪt] 擊中
- **knock over**
  [kɑːk ˈoʊ.və]
  撞倒；使震驚
- **be defeated** [bi: dɪˈfiːtɪd]
  被打敗

p. 42

戰後，克羅納斯遠走他鄉。
宙斯將戰敗的泰坦神驅逐到地心，
由百手怪看管。
宙斯與其他神祇共分天下，
他成為天地之神，也是眾神之王。
波賽墩則掌管海洋，
海地士則成為冥界之神。

- **far away** [fɑ:r əˋweɪ]
  遠離
- **sent** [sent] 打發；派遣
  （send的過去式）
- **share A with B**
  [ʃer eɪ wɪð bi:]
  和A分享B
- **heaven** [ˋhev.ən]
  天堂；天國

 p. 44

在奧林帕斯，
一共有十二位神祇，
他們居住在希臘的奧林帕斯仙境上。
這些神祇掌管大自然，
啟發著人類。

- **brought** [brɑ:t]
  帶來（bring的過去式）
- **idea** [aɪˋdɪə]
  意見；見解

p. 45

父親說完故事，
便和伊卡一起回家。
多年後，伊卡長大成人。
一天夜裡，
伊卡和兒子坐在同一座山丘上，
述說著同樣的故事。
今晚，在希臘的這座山丘上，
也有一對父子，
再次述說著同樣的故事。

- **told** [toʊld]
  告訴（tell的過去式）
- **went** [went]
  去（go的過去式）
- **go home** [goʊ hoʊm]
  回家
- **later** [leɪtə]
  較晚；過後；後來
- **same** [seɪm] 相同
- **tonight** [tə`naɪt]
  今晚
- **be retold** [bi: ri:toʊld]
  再次被述說

# 閱讀測驗

p. 46 ~ p. 48

## Part1

※閱讀下列問題並選出最適當的答案。

1. 在希臘羅馬神話的故事中,最早出現的是什麼?
   (A) 宙斯　　　(B) 蓋亞
   (C) 渾沌　　　(D) 大地

   答案 (C)

2. 車輪眼巨人有幾隻眼睛?
   (A) 1　　　　(B) 2
   (C) 10　　　(D) 100

   答案 (A)

3. 克羅納斯對他的孩子們做了什麼,使他們無法反抗他?
   (A) 他把他們送到奧林帕斯仙境去了。
   (B) 他把他們送到地球的中心去了。
   (C) 他吃了他們。
   (D) 他把他們囚禁了起來。

   答案 (C)

25

4. 大洋氏的女兒是誰?

    (A) 守誓河        (B) 赫拉

    (C) 雅典娜        (D) 羅貝塔

    答案 (A)


5. 誰是阿瑪爾夏?

    (A) 宙斯的母親    (B) 一位山羊女神

    (C) 統治神的人    (C) 宙斯的太太

    答案 (B)

## Part2

※閱讀下列句子並圈選。

6. 車輪眼巨人和克羅納斯都是烏拉諾斯的兒子。

    ( True )    False        答案 True

7. 蓋亞在洞穴中照顧小宙斯。

    True    ( False )        答案 False

8. 宙斯變成了冥界之神。

    True    ( False )        答案 False

9. 車輪眼巨人把三叉戟給了海地士。

    True    ( False )        答案 False

10. 宙斯住在希臘的奧林帕斯仙境上。

    ( True )    False        答案 True

故事原著作者 **Thomas Bulfinch**

Without a knowledge of mythology much of the elegant literature of our own language cannot be understood and appreciated.

缺少了神話知識，就無法了解和透徹語言的文學之美。

—*Thomas Bulfinch*

Thomas Bulfinch（1796-1867），出生於美國麻薩諸塞州的Newton，隨後全家移居波士頓，父親爲知名的建築師Charles Bulfinch。他在求學時期，曾就讀過一些優異的名校，並於1814年畢業於哈佛。

畢業後，執過教鞭，爾後從商，但經濟狀況一直未能穩定。1837年，在銀行擔任一般職員，以此爲終身職業。後來開始進一步鑽研古典文學，成爲業餘作家，一生未婚。

1855年，時值59歲，出版了奠立其作家地位的名作*The Age of Fables*，書中蒐集希臘羅馬神話，廣受歡迎。此書後來與日後出版的 *The Age of Chivalry*（1858）和 *Legends of Charlemagne*（1863），合集更名爲 *Bulfinch's Mythology*。

本系列書系，即改編自 *The Age of Fable*。Bulfinch 著寫本書時，特地以成年大眾爲對象，以將古典文學引介給一般大眾。*The Age of Fable* 堪稱十九世紀的羅馬神話故事的重要代表著作，其中有很多故事來源，來自Bulfinch自己對奧維德（Ovid）的《變形記》（*Metamorphoses*）的翻譯。

■Bulfinch的著作

1. Hebrew Lyrical History.
2. The Age of Fable: Or Stories of Gods and Heroes.
3. The Age of Chivalry.
4. The Boy Inventor: A Memoir of Matthew Edwards, Mathematical-Instrument Maker.
5. Legends of Charlemagne.
6. Poetry of the Age of Fable.
7. Shakespeare Adapted for Reading Classes.
8. Oregon and Eldorado.
9. Bulfinch's Mythology: Age of Fable, Age of Chivalry, Legends of Charlemagne.